AF674304

Canapé Collection: Laita

Atreyo Mitra was born in 1994, in Kolkata, India. An early fascination towards World Cinema, Brit-pop music, and postmodern literature, fuelled Mitra's attraction towards storytelling.

In 2017, Mitra graduated from *Srishti Institute of Art, Design, and Technology* with a major in Film. In 2018, Mitra continued his studies at *Vancouver Film School* with a focus in Screenwriting for Films, Television, and Games.

Canapé Collection: Laita is Mitra's debut short story collection. Mitra is currently based out of Mumbai where he continues to work on his short stories and upcoming novels.

This is a work of fiction. Names, characters, places, and incidents either are the product of the author's imagination or are used fictitiously. Any resemblance to actual persons, living, or dead, events, or locales is entirely coincidental.

Independently published in 2019
Andheri, Mumbai, Maharashtra, 400102

First paperback edition May 2019

Book design by Dev Ethan Valladares

Book edited by Rhea Iyer

ISBN 978-93-5361-489-8

Canapé
Collective

ATREYO MITRA

Canapé Collection: Laita

To Ma, Baba, & Dada.

Contents

Acknowledgements

There was a battle that played in my head, a borderline war if I may, over the simple decision of whether or not to include an acknowledgements section in this book.

Yes, without a doubt, this book would not have been possible without the help of several talented individuals, in fact, when I say 'several', the numbers may just be high enough to double up the page count of this humble collection.

However, there are certain people without whom these stories might've never been published, perhaps never even written.

Thankfully, if you are reading this, then these stories have indeed been published, and I'm glad to have had the following people play an integral role in the creation of this collection.

This list, just like any and all acknowledgement lists that I may prepare in my life will begin with my family. If it weren't for *Riddhit Mitra*, *Sujata Mitra*, and *Indrajit Mitra*, I would definitely not have written any of these stories. Our families shape who we are and what we do as people.

Every now and then, in this funny world of ours, you'll find a rebellious child pick up a pair of drumsticks, a paintbrush, or a Chef's knife (hopefully with the intention to stab, and nothing beyond that).

In all of these moments, I can hear a million hearts break as they cry out, "Ah! Why couldn't you have picked up something with a career?"

I don't have a reassuring or definitive answer to that question. Some people are born leaders, some are fantastic at chess, some people love following the rules, and a lot of them love breaking them. Some people are reckless explorers, some people, stern disciplinarians.

Personally, I'm still not sure what kind am I, but I thank my family for supporting me despite my interminable confusion.

Next up I would like to thank the *57th Writing Class* of *Vancouver Film School*. Stories had been just mere ideas on a page, like amorphous creatures struggling to breathe in an unwelcoming planet. All that changed when I came across this eclectic bunch of misfits who would read and reread each other's works, selflessly helping one another grow at the craft that we all love.

Jonny DiVito, Jackie Agnew, and Tom Cuypers, if it weren't for you three crazy monkeys, I would've never gained the confidence to put out my work for the world to see like I'm doing today. You were the push that I needed to take this first step, and then think about the second step after 'a' pint at the *340*.

It would be absolutely remiss of me to not mention the people who have directly contributed to *Canapé Collection: Laita*, and without whom this book would not be what it is today.

Dev Ethan Valladares, firstly, I thank you for simply being there as a friend with whom I can stay up till an unhealthy hour of dawn and somehow still feel as though the conversation is only just beginning. You're one of the smartest, most talented, and quintessentially unique people I know, and I am simply honoured to have you as a part of the Canapé Collective.

Rhea Iyer, I was nothing short of ecstatic when I got to know that you would be editing my book. To look at any form of art and to appraise it objectively is undoubtedly one of the most challenging things one can do. It was absolutely imperative for me to find someone I could trust with my work, and for that person to be you, I simply couldn't be any happier.

Finally, I would like to thank *Nehal Vyas and Trisha Bhattacharya*, who, ever since the second year of college, have been the most reliable and unfiltered critics of my work. You kept me grounded when I was drifting aimlessly in the tumultuous sky, focused when I was busy getting lost in the clouds, and motivated when I ran out of aerial analogies.

Once again, thank you all for being a part of the first book by the *Canapé Collective.* We've embarked on an adventure, unaware of where it'll lead us, but as long as we're together, I'm sure we're headed for the sunset.

Atreyo Mitra

A Fictional Introduction

If my memory serves right, it had all started with a test. In school, we used to have these tests daily. Mondays would be Mathematics, Tuesdays would be Science, and it was probably a Wednesday when it came turn for English. I was about six years old at the time and coming from a Bengali family, it didn't matter what your age was; If you're scoring low grades in your exams, you're unquestionably on the wrong side of history.

Despair, anger, and hopelessness spread through the house as I brought my disastrous result back home. I had scored eighteen out of twenty-five in English. There were eighteen ways things could've gone worse, but that was the *Optimist* in me speaking (ever since that day, he's not welcome in the house anymore).

As my Mother wondered where it had all gone wrong, my brother conjured up ideas as to how I could've improved on my English. He finally came up with a possible solution. "You've got to watch *good* English movies, and you've got to read *good* English books." He said confidently. It didn't help. Believe it or not, watching movies before an exam does not guarantee great reward.

Like an invisible evil, our three unwelcome guests, despair, anger, and hopelessness, continued to spread. My brother spent countless hours in his basement lab where he brewed new methods that would, in turn, rectify my inability to score 'well' in these weekly English tests.

This time, he said, "I've figured it all out! I had botched my calculations before, a tiny error in the algorithm. But now I know what you need to do. You need to write!"

Suddenly, the invisible crowd that resided in my house broke into a loud and ecstatic applause. My mother too loved this idea so much that she suggested I write one short story every day.

"Would my English really improve if I wrote a short story daily?" I thought to myself. I wasn't even sure if I wanted to improve my English. I was a born a rebel, you see, and school tests just weren't my cup of tea. However, it would definitely be a problem if Mom kicked me out of the house, so I decided, *What the hell, let's write some short stories.*

My grades never improved. For sake of consistency, I decided to lower my Math and Science grades as well, so that my English grades wouldn't feel so lonely all the time. However, if anything good came out of all of this, it would have to be the fact that I had now become addicted to penning down short stories. Ask any smoker, alcoholic, or video gamer what cigarettes, alcohol, or video games mean to them.

"I don't really know what it means, but what I do know is that it's an essential part of my being now." Is what they would say, or it is at least what I think I would want to say if anyone ever poses me the very same question with respect to writing stories. I had written several stories. Hundreds if not thousands.

As I write this today, I have absolutely no idea where all these stories have gone. Like that friend who one day abruptly disappears from your life without even saying goodbye. Don't you just hate it when that happens? I do too, which is why I have decided to unearth the few old stories of mine that still remain, and let them out, to breathe life in the real world.

With *Canapé Collection: Laita*, I have finally released the first six of the select few stories that survived out of the thousands. Allow me to take a quick moment and sincerely thank you for picking up my book. I wish nothing more than for you to enjoy the six tales that *Laita* has to offer.

Since this is my first time doing this, I'm going to be honest with you. Most of this introduction has been altered from the true events for dramatic purposes. Believe it or not, my brother did not have a basement laboratory, and the 'invisible crowd' that resided in my house was actually just a singular invisible man, named Timmy.

Here's to you, Timmy.
This first one's for you.

The Morning After

I woke up next to a beautiful, naked stranger, but stranger still was the apartment I woke up in. Unlike my own apartment, the walls of this room were clean, there was a carefully organised study table beside the window, and the bed I lay on was a real bed, not the flimsy mattress on the floor that I'd gotten so accustomed to.

What had happened last night? What were the events that had led me to this exact moment? I tried to remember, but my memory failed me; it wasn't just the *yesterday* that I was forgetting. It felt as though I'd also lost something more... fundamental. It was a very unfamiliar world I'd found myself in, and I needed to escape it before it was too late.

I took the 8:53 fast train to Andheri and within an hour I was back in my own studio. In a city like Mumbai, an hour was the standard time it would take to reach anywhere, close by or far away. Distance was not a determinant.

In the studio, I gazed at the painting in front of me and the painting, *Curtains,* returned it. All my paintings were extensions of myself; within all of them, a piece of my identity — in a way I kept myself rooted with every piece that made its way to completion.

Curtains was a work-in-progress and after about forty minutes, I knew exactly what it was lacking. *Baby Powder White*. My picture was bereft of the purity that this colour would doubtlessly provide.

Except, there was a problem because my palette was lacking it. The colour, I mean. I reached for my paint box and rummaged through the countless bottles of paint. No luck there, either. After a rigorous search of my apartment, I came to the conclusion that my *white* had either been misplaced or god forbid, *stolen*.

I had a bad habit of pocketing my colours while using them, so I convinced myself that I'd lost my colour somewhere in the blur of yesterday's memories.

I hopped onto the train once again. After about an hour, I sat myself down in my baby sister's dorm room, which had been the last place I remembered visiting.

"You can't recall anything?" she responded, cackling at my troubles. "Boy, you must've gotten sloshed."

"I went to the bar?" I asked, despite having already known the answer.

"You said you were heading there to meet a few of your friends. And this was back when you'd been sober!" She laughed again. I joined in. It felt nice to hear her make light of the situation. Such would not have been the case if she'd known that I had lost my *Baby Powder White*.

I told myself that it wasn't an important detail, and that I didn't need to disclose it. It wasn't like I was embarrassed, or ashamed of my carelessness. It's not like it was a big deal to lose one's Baby Powder White, was it?

'No, these sort of things happen every day.' I consoled myself as my laugh turned awkward and I hastily shut up.

The bar too turned out to be a total bust. The bartender lady seemed to remember my face and pointed me to my table from yesterday, which was thankfully vacant at this hour. After a thorough search, I accepted defeat.

With my tail between my legs, I made my way out, when suddenly, the bartender asked, "What exactly are you looking for?"

"I lost a small bottle of colour last night." I sighed.

"By any chance, was it Baby Powder White?"

I was amazed. "Yes!" I exclaimed. "Do you have it?"

"Not exactly, but I've got several bottles of that in the 'Lost and Found'. It appears to be quite a popular item to forget in our bar." She gave me a kind smile. "If you'd like, you could just take one."

Back in my apartment, I gazed helplessly at *Curtains,* who gazed back with judgment. I could feel a piece of myself fading away, like an unpreserved work of art.

In my hand, I held some stranger's empty bottle of *Baby Powder White*. I should have checked the contents at the bar itself, but it didn't matter anymore. Something told me that even if I had opened up every single one of those bottles individually, they would have all proven to be empty.

I continued to gaze helplessly at *Curtains*. My identity had depended on completing this painting, but I guess that wasn't going to happen anymore, which now begged the question — *so who was I, anyway?*

"At least fade away in your own trousers," whispered a voice in my head. I looked down. He was right. I had never seen these muddy khakis before. I must've left mine at the stranger's apartment. Perhaps it was time to pay her another visit.

The beautiful, naked stranger's name was Dahlia. She wasn't particularly excited to see me again, but she didn't seem displeased either, so I figured she was friendly.

Upon asking, she went to the bed I'd spent the night on and pulled out my bottle of *Baby Powder White* from underneath the sheets.

"I put your pants for a wash," she said. "I'll bring it over later."

"Did I give you my address?" I wondered.

"I don't recall."

"There's a Cafe Coffee Day next to my apartment?"

"It's too expensive. Don't you have coffee at home?"

We made arrangements to meet at my studio the next day for coffee. After that, I made my way back to Andheri.

Back at my studio, I painted for hours as I devoted myself to fixing *Curtains*. But something was amiss.

My Baby Powder White felt more like muddy alabaster. No matter how hard I tried, my picture refused to achieve the brightness I had been striving for. It was seven o'clock at night and my time had long run out. Something in me had faded, just like the purity that I had once envisioned for *Curtains*. My relationship with this painting had changed; Somewhere between the blur of last night and the time I opened my eyes, we had stopped resonating with each other.

'No colour can complete this piece,' I thought to myself. Suddenly feeling bereft of any motivation to see it to the end, I picked up the canvas and threw it out the studio window.

I placed a fresh canvas on the easel and reached for a clean brush. My movements were fluid, the brush strokes, organic; giving rise to striking, fearless swathes of colour, and the overlap of accidental splatters only adding to the animated chaos.

Hours passed, and my lips pulled up into a smile as the canvas began to show me something I once again resonated with; every canvas, a mirror in tune. Gone were those subdued tones of *Curtains*. *Baby Powder White* became dispensable. Raging bold, bright, and violent — reds, yellows, and violets — my canvas breathed new life, and it needed a name.

Images from today flashed through my mind, of the immaculate room I'd woken up in, of the strangeness I'd felt as I had opened my eyes in the morning — I could see them on the canvas in front of me. Tomorrow, that feeling would be lost forever — I would meet Dahlia for coffee, and we would become acquaintances, or even friends, and I would exchange that strangeness for familiarity, and again, something would alter within me. My canvas, however, would continue to remember that feeling.

I turned the canvas and scribbled on both my name and the painting's. *The Morning After.*

A sense of accomplishment flooded within me as I stared at the painting, finally satisfied, when —

I squinted.

I tilted my head. For a good ten minutes, I studied it from every angle, and then I *saw* it.

There was still something missing, something that prevented it from achieving completion. The bold strokes of red, yellow, and violet were like three islands with no bridge to connect one to the other. *The Morning After* demanded a fourth colour, and I had absolutely no clue as to what that colour could be.

Despondent, I tried to shove my hands into my pockets when I realized that both of them were stuffed to the brim with little bottles of paint. I quickly began to take them out, god forbid they too suffered the same fate as *Baby Powder White*.

After all the reds, yellows, and violets had been successfully extracted, I finally pulled out the very last one. I turned it in my hands to read the label, and it just so happened to be *Night Sky Black.* One look at the pigment and I understood that I had found the bridge I'd been looking for. I did not question how this colour had found its way into my pocket. Perhaps it was fate. More likely, I had a poor memory.

I could've finished the painting right then and there. The answer was right there, in my hand. The canvas too, having witnessed the unfortunate fate of its elder brother, was impatient. It couldn't wait to attain completion.

Unfortunately, after hours of work, my body was tired and my mind was exhausted. Where exactly the *Night Sky Black* needed to go on my canvas was still a mystery, and I decided that it wasn't going to be solved tonight. I went to put the bottle in with the rest of them when my fingers suddenly tightened across the surface.

For some reason, I was reluctant to let it out of my sight. 'It's obviously special,' I thought with uncertainty. 'So vital to this piece — what if I lost it in the studio's clutter?'

Without this colour, there would be no *Morning After.* I put the bottle back in my pocket, determined to keep it close, confident that I wouldn't repeat the same mistake twice.

To celebrate the day's productivity, I headed for the bar.

"You're back again, I see," said the bartender as I took a seat by the counter. "What'll it be then?"

“Same thing,” I replied. “Whiskey ginger.”

“No one joining you?” She grinned as she began to prepare my drink.

“Just here to wind down. It’s been a long day.”

“One of those, eh?” she commiserated as she presented me with my Whiskey Ginger. “And how did it go with the *Baby Powder White?*”

“Turns out that I didn’t need it after all,” I said, taking a sip. “I’m working on something different now. Thanks for the help, though.”

“No problem. So you’re a painter, is it?”

“Almost,” I quipped. “Still struggling, so I guess I haven’t yet qualified for the title.”

“Welcome to the club,” she laughed.

I raised my drink for a toast and she clinked it with an empty glass before slipping away to tend to the other patrons. I felt for the bottle of paint through my trouser pocket to ensure I still had it on me.

Music blared through the speakers, and I allowed myself to sink into it. It was *Once in a Lifetime* by *The Talking Heads,* and it was loud enough to eclipse every conversation, but I thankfully didn’t intend on having any.

As I sipped on my drink, I wondered what the bartender was struggling to achieve. As I crunched on the ice, I wondered what anyone in ‘the club’ was struggling to achieve. Was it even going to be worth it, or was it all for nothing?

But then the paint again made its weight known against my thigh, and I decided to discard these needless, existential thoughts. I had to focus on what was truly important.

The morning after.

The Craft Of Ignorance

I'd read the text message late last night. It was the primary reason I'd felt sleep deprived through the morning, and spent most of my afternoon in utter anxiety. The message kept popping up in my head:

Hi, Richa! Long time. I'm in town (have been for a while, actually). I will be going to a concert tomorrow at The Golden Yak. Wanna meet up? It's at six.

It was from Jishu — the only person in my contacts who could use a comma before an 'actually' that was inside a parenthetical, for a text message.

On my phone, I had his number saved as *Shuie*, a little nickname that I'd given him. I was the only one who would call him that, but that had been back when we were still together.

It'd been almost a year since we'd broken up. Why did I still have his number saved on my phone? I told myself that I'd simply forgotten to erase it. Last night, I regretted not having done so. I never would've checked a message from an unknown number, as opposed to the innocuously sweet-sounding Shuie.

It was already 4 o'clock and I still hadn't made up my mind on whether or not I should go. I wondered which band was performing, but didn't find any information about upcoming performances in the pub. Nothing on the internet, nothing on the news. Was it all word of mouth? In this day and age? Astonishing.

I wondered why he'd been in town 'for a while'. Had he permanently shifted to Mumbai? Found a job here? Why had he left Gujarat? Had he been fired? Unlikely. After all, he was a smart, hardworking, and honest guy, one of the nicest people I had ever met, and possibly the last person I would expect to get fired from a job.

Since the night before, my instincts had been constantly nagging me. They told me to go and meet him. However, the memory was still fresh and the wound was something I'd hoped to avoid letting resurface.

I still remembered the weeks I had spent just lying in bed. I'd done nothing. All I'd thought about was how my life had come to a premature end. I'd cried incessantly, except for when I didn't, where instead, I'd worked out excessively. The crying suffered a very slow death. It'd felt like a lifetime. It probably had been.

Unlike the tears, the over-exercising had come to an abrupt end. One day, I realized that there was no one I was looking to impress with my physique, and that I certainly didn't see myself as the fitness type. The whole thing had been an utter mistake.

Soon after, I found myself a job with Kiran, a childhood friend. In addition to being my employer, she also happened to be my roommate. The pay wasn't much, but I was able to sustain myself by living frugally.

I stared at the elephant in the room as though I was sharing history with the mammal. A part of me said that I should go, while another said that I definitely shouldn't. As the clock ticked away, the pressure to make a decision grew heavier. My anxiety developed a voice of its own. Stronger and more confident than the voices of my instincts and memory, it needled, "Richa, you must go. If you don't, he'll probably think you're still not over him."

Those bold and confident words were exactly what I needed. There was absolutely no way I was going to let Shuie think I was still heartbroken over him. I wasn't. The crying Richa, maybe. The over-exercising Richa, perhaps her too. But this Richa right here, today, was in no way agonizing over a lost love. I decided to go.

I was on the way to my room with different outfit ideas flitting through my head when the doorbell rang. I hadn't been expecting anyone at this hour in the afternoon.

Had he come here to meet me? As far as I could recall, he hadn't been the impatient type. Could he have come to take me away? I imagined us eloping to a small town full of art and greenery. Life would be simple. We'd live like total bohemians. Nothing would be manufactured in this new world of ours. Everything would be organic, from the milk we'd drink to the soaps we'd use. The two of us would be in each other's arms for hours on end, pondering over the pages of a novel we'd be reading together, wondering to ourselves if life would ever be this good again.

With a dreamy sigh, I opened the door to find the local carpenter staring back at me with a strained smile. I would later learn that this was simply what his face looked like. He was clad in a gaudy yellow shirt, torn at the armpits. Complimenting the shirt were a pair of muddied jeans.

"Ma'am," he said. "I've brought the mirror."

The delivery had come early. The mirror hadn't been due to arrive for another two days. This, I realized, was not a coincidence. Doubtless, a sign sent to me from a land beyond human control.

"How long will it take for you to set it up?" I asked the carpenter as I leaned against the door jamb.

"Forty-five minutes, ma'am," he said before adding, "Four hundred rupees." Apparently, signs from the universe didn't come cheap.

I showed the carpenter to the living room and he immediately got to work. Four hundred rupees to set up a mirror was simply criminal, but I wasn't in the mood for an argument.

The images of possible outfits for the evening had all but disappeared. I couldn't leave now. Kiran had forgotten to lock up her room again, and she wouldn't take kindly to finding out that I'd trusted the apartment to the local carpenter.

I began to calculate: with a forty-five minute wait for the carpenter to finish up, some time to get ready, and then finally actually leaving for the Golden Yak — it would be five-ish by the time I managed to catch a cab. In the evening traffic, it would easily take me an hour and a half to reach the venue, which was too late.

It was decided then. I would message Shuie the following:

Hey Jishu, something came up all of a sudden, and I, unfortunately, won't be able to make it to the

concert tonight. I was really hoping to meet you. Anyway, have fun at the show! Next time, give me an earlier heads up, yeah?

This, after all, was the truth and in no respect an excuse.

I was convinced that the universe had seen fit to make the difficult decision on my behalf. It was as though something far more powerful than myself was constantly watching over me, and that I could trust it to have my back. That is, of course, until Kiran's unlocked door opened and out she walked.

"Oh, good, the carpenter's here," said Kiran. Upon seeing me with my phone in hand as I stood aimlessly in the middle of the room, she continued, "Listen, I'm in the apartment for the day, so feel free to leave if you've made plans or anything of the sort."

Hence, it turned out that the powerful protector and well-wisher who ostensibly had my back was nothing more than an imaginary creature that I'd made up.

Out of all days, why did Kiran have to be in the apartment today? Usually, she'd bunk at her boyfriend's studio. It wasn't uncommon for her to go out on a drunken spree that would last till the wee hours of morning. She'd end up passing out on the couch of some friend whose house would be in closest proximity to the pub.

Come to think of it, I'd never seen Kiran saunter around the apartment with disheveled hair, clad in shorts before. She just wasn't that person. Always dressed to kill, an ephemeral and sociable woman, either going to work or on her way to an enviable party. So why did she have to be in the apartment today?

"So, got any plans, Richa?" she asked, probably in an attempt to kill the awkward silence.

"How come you're in the apartment?" I cried out impetuously.

"Where else am I supposed to be?" she shot back.

"I don't mean it that way! It's just that I thought I was alone here, and now all my plans are ruined."

"You wanted to be alone here, with the carpenter?"

"I didn't mean that either! There's nothing between me and the carpenter!"

"Well, that's a relief. What in the world are you so worked up about, babe?" She said, in a tone that reignited my trust in her as a friend.

Of late, it had become quite difficult for me to see Kiran as someone I could confide in. I found myself in situations where the hierarchy of a corporate institution lingered scrupulously above us. Professionally speaking, she was my boss, and I, her subordinate loyal employee. But it didn't have to be this way, right? I decided to tell her everything. After all, we were friends, and friends share their troubles with each other.

"Shuie messaged me last night. He wants to meet. I can't decide whether or not I should go." I said.

"Shuie?" She wondered to herself for a second or two. I left her brewing in the confusion until she finally figured out whom I was talking about.

"Oh! You mean Jishu! You should totally go and see him. He was such a sweetie!"

"Yes, but he was also my boyfriend. And we broke up a year ago, hello? Doesn't that mean anything?" I told her pointedly.

"A year? Has it really been that long? I'm sure he's over you by now. Aren't you?"

"Of course, I am!" My ego retorted.

"Then you should go. Otherwise, he might think that you're still not over him. Then he'll start pitying you and whatnot. Trust me, it'll get messy. The last thing you want is to make him think that you're weak. Am I right?"

"I think so."

"Plus, it might be fun, you never know. He was a nice guy after all."

"He was a nice guy," I repeated and confirmed her statement in a tone that deemed it unnecessary for any appraisal regarding Shuie's niceness.

Kiran gave me a warm and comforting smile. I couldn't tell if it was a sincere smile, for it lasted less than a second. Barely a moment passed until she was once again disappearing into her room, slamming the door on my face before I could even consider returning her smile. It was as though someone had given you a hug, but you couldn't be sure if it'd been a gesture of affection or if they'd intentionally bumped into you. I convinced myself that it was indeed a hug.

I went into my room in order to get dressed for the Golden Yak. En route to my closet, I realized my state of vacillation. I had once again changed my mind and was now convinced to go.

On opening my cupboard, as if it were fate, my eyes automatically fell on a pretty summer dress I'd bought a couple of years ago but had never gotten the chance to wear. It was a beige cotton dress, complete with some tastefully bright and colourful embroidery at the hem.

'I'd love to wear this' I thought to myself. A guilty afterthought followed, 'I'm sure Shuie would like it as well.'

'No!' I told myself sternly. I had to be my own teacher in this situation. This was by no means a special occasion. Just two old friends meeting each other after a protracted period of time. I decided to go with something more casual, perhaps a plaid shirt and some light blue jeans. But, I further debated, wouldn't that be far too casual for an up and coming joint like The Golden Yak? The barrage of thoughts continued. What if they don't let me enter? Would it have an adverse effect on my self-confidence? What if Shuie refuses to recognize me? He'd never. Would he?

I decided to put the outfit decision on hold. The sky seemed exorbitantly cloudy and one could feel the dampness in the air. Bereft of the sun, my summer dress just wouldn't feel right on me. I would become a hanger advertising the dress for others to judge whether or not they'd wear such a thing in more appropriate weather conditions.

I bent down to take a look at which shoes I should wear for the occasion. On noticing the now dried and dirty mud stuck to my favourite black heels, my heart underwent a rapid freefall. A quick glance at my other options and my heart sank even further. I definitely wasn't going to wear red flip flops to the venue. Neither was I keen on putting on my torn blue Nike sneakers. The black heels were my only option, and they were exactly what would've suited the occasion. They didn't exude any form of ostentation, nor were they, by any means, perfunctory. They were the perfect choice.

Dumbfounded, I stared at the decrepit shoes and couldn't help but feel as though I was looking at a reflection of my own soul.

'This is exactly how I feel right now,' I thought to myself. 'Like a forgotten, helpless, and repulsive pair of shoes. I am obviously still not over him.' And of course, how could I be? He was, after all, such a nice guy.

The teacher within me resurfaced and advised me to abandon that little dream I'd been entertaining. Nothing good would come out of seeing him again. The wisest move was to protect myself from situations like this that threatened emotional damage.

This is when my cell phone began to ring. I looked at the screen and was immediately reassured that I'd made the right call by choosing not to go. On the screen, I saw the name 'Prabhu' flash. He was doubtlessly calling me to make plans for the evening.

My relationship with Prabhu had begun when I'd met him at an office event about seven months ago. His simple nature and absent-minded naïveté had somehow managed to take a firm hold of my heart, but unfortunately, he lacked the confidence to approach me and ask me out. He was a Pondicherry boy and spoke in broken English. Although it made him very insecure, I found his accent quite endearing.

Sadly, he never plucked up the courage to approach me. It was I who eventually went up to him and asked him out for a cup of coffee. That was the first and last time I took initiative in our relationship, for after that fateful day, Prabhu began to see himself as some sort of protector of mine. He would often make the plans to go out for drinks or catch the occasional show at the theatre. He had also been a very good listener, especially when I would ramble on about my heartbreak with Shuie.

"Don't worry, I won't let anything like that happen to you ever again," he would tell me.

I picked up the call, and with diligent alacrity said, "Hey Prabhu, what's up?"

"Richa, you're not going to meet him, are you?" he asked rather aggressively.

"What? How did you…"

"Boss told me. She called me a while back, but I didn't have any balance. I thought you'd obviously call me for advice, but when you didn't, I had to put money into my phone and call you instead."

"First of all, Kiran had no right! Secondly, I'm sorry I made you put money in your phone, Prabhu, but this is a personal matter that I intend to resolve on my own, which is why I didn't call you. But it doesn't matter! I'm not going." I said confidently.

"That's smart. He's a pathetic human being, I hope you remember that."

"Geez, okay, what are you, my Dad?"

"I'm your boyfriend."

"Look, we like each other, but let's not start putting labels on it, okay?"

"What do you mean?"

"Like boyfriend, girlfriend, and whatnot. Makes me feel like you'll propose to me any second now!" I said to which followed a long and awkward pause from his end.

"But you *are* my girlfriend. Okay, I'm willing to put the marriage discussion aside for now, but you've got to take into account all the things that I've done for you, asking for nothing in return. All I want from you is that you promise not to go to that loser, and even this I'm saying for your own good, Richa."

"First of all, let's kick that marriage discussion out of the park, secondly if there's anyone who controls my life, it's me! I don't need your permission to meet someone. I can meet whoever the hell I want, understand?"

"Just calm down. You don't wanna say anything irrational now, do you?"

"Yeah? It's funny. Before you'd called, I had already decided to not go, but now thanks to you... you know what? I'm definitely going. Bye, Prabhu." I immediately cut the call. I felt like throwing my phone out the window, but this one was quite expensive and my paycheque wasn't due for another two weeks.

I stormed into Kiran's room. She was watching some Mexican soap opera. I donned my fiercest flare and began to yell at her furiously. "I can't believe you told Prabhu about Shuie! I trusted you, and you just went and spewed everything out to probably the last person I wanted involved in any of this. You were way out of line, Kiran, way outta —"

"Relax, babe! I thought Prabhu and you were dating, and obviously it's quite serious so I simply assumed that he should know."

"No!" I exclaimed. "It's not serious! Why would you even think that?"

"Well, he was looking up diamond rings on Amazon all through last week. I thought I'd tell him to keep all this personal stuff outside the office, but then, just the thought of you two getting hitched made me all giddy inside, so I let the whole thing slide."

I just stood there and stared at Kiran, unable to find the right words to respond with.

"Plus, I thought that you were having trouble deciding whether or not to go," she continued. "So I thought, 'Hey! What's better than two minds?' Three minds, of course!"

"No! Have you never heard about the too many cooks and soup thing? It's never a good idea to…" I trailed off, my words reducing to incoherence as my gaze landed on a beautiful pair of green stilettos in the corner of Kiran's room.

'Those would go perfectly with my summer dress.' I thought.

"What soup are you talking about?" Kiran asked, breaking me out of my reverie.

"You know what soup," I replied in the best irate tone that I could muster.

"What do you want from me? Fine, *I'm sorry*. There, happy?"

"No. As punishment for intruding into my personal life, you need to let me borrow your stilettos… please?"

Her eyebrows rose. "If it makes you feel any better, sure, go ahead," she replied indifferently. "Just a warning though, they will kill your feet." And then she returned to her soap opera.

I quickly grabbed the stilettos, rushed into my bedroom to put on the beige summer dress, and grinned at my reflection in the dressing table mirror.

I couldn't remember the last time I'd thought of myself as an attractive girl. And looking at me now, I understood that there was no wrong weather condition for a handsome summer dress. Unless, of course, if it rained.

And sure enough, just as the ominous thought crossed my mind, it began to pour mercilessly, dampening all my hopes of visiting Shuie.

It drew to a conclusion with the next message I received on my phone. The name Shuie flashed on my screen and I clicked on the blurb.

The band cancelled. No show tonight at The Gold Yak because of the rain.

Hence, things were back in their rightful place, thanks to this unexpected downpour. Perhaps someone was indeed making the right decisions for me, after all. However, I had to admit, I had been looking forward to a relaxed evening with an old friend, with some live music and a few drinks.

Now that everything was over, no more did I have to worry about looking brave, strong, weak, or whatever.

In retrospect, I felt a bit silly to have ever had let such anxiety control my decision over something as banal as meeting an old friend for a fun evening.

I decided to reply back to Shuie, something along the lines of:

Sure, maybe next time! Tell me when you're free.

No, the alacrity was simply too apparent. Perhaps:

Yeah! You can say that the rain totally stole the show tonight.

I liked that. It was humorous and didn't reveal any emotion from my side whatsoever.

I went on to type the message which I had so very brilliantly constructed in my head when suddenly, I saw that Shuie had sent yet another text.

Looks like the rain stole the show tonight! Ha! Anyway just out of curiosity, would you like to come over to my place? Long time. We could catch up over a couple of beers.

All of a sudden, matters didn't seem as innocuous as I had been picturing them to be. Shuie had invited me to his house, and I had no idea what to make of it. I began to calculate again: if I were to leave now, I would probably reach his place after six. That certainly couldn't be considered an *innocent* hour. This was definitely no longer about two old friends spending some time together, but about two separated lovers making the tough decision to try and reconcile. The exact extent of reconciliation was still foggy.

I wondered whether or not we would end up having sex. If we did, would it be more of a one-time thing? Or would it entail something protracted, perhaps the rebirth of our relationship? Eventually, we would just move in together, meet each other's parents, then marriage, a baby — possibly two, a boy and a girl — and following that, of course, a Labrador; or was he more of a cat person? Would we sustain it long enough or would it end in an acrimonious divorce

— hopefully, a pleasant one. What would it be like for us to grow old together? Probably beautiful. Definitely annoying.

I stopped for a second and realized that I had spiralled far too deep into my imagination. First thing's first — should I stay, or should I go?

I felt immense relief over the fact that Shuie had invited me over to his place, not particularly because I wanted to pay him a visit, but because I realized how flawed the both of us were. Up until then, I had been unable to glimpse his intentions, but now it was abundantly clear to me. He too was not over me.

Once again, like a magnet, every instinct of mine pulled me towards taking the first crazy step that would eventually lead me to his doorstep. However, I was painfully aware of my recent past. It was a torment so abrasive, the memory of which resisted that very first step with all its might.

It said, "If you go, it'll destroy everything that you've built over this past year. Everything that is holding you together right now is going to fall apart, and you will not be able to get up again." Won't I? No, definitely not. Not again.

I was going to have to say goodbye to Prabhu, and he most definitely wasn't going to take it well. Had he actually been planning to propose? Had he already bought the ring? Dammit. This was going to affect my diligence towards work as well. I'd never been one to strike a satisfactory balance between the professional and the personal. A persistent, passionate fool since birth. That's me. Always have been.

My eyes were wide open. I knew that if I actually were to go to Shuie today, it was definitely going to be the stupider decision.

'This, of course, wouldn't be the first time I'd be acting like an idiot,' I thought to myself as I recalled how and why I had left Shuie in the first place. It had hit him unawares, like a silent tsunami.

A year ago, I'd told him that it was time we call it quits. Why had I said that? He had often asked me the reason *why* and I'd never give him the same answer. Sometimes I would forget what I had told him before. Sometimes I would just feel as though there was a better, a more honest response than the one I had given him previously.

I'd feel terrible when he'd show up at my doorstep in the pretence of something ridiculous, like "I just wanted to see how you're doing," or "I just want to clarify a few more things about why we didn't work out."

This eventually led me to take a more hostile attitude towards him, which consequently drove him farther away from me. I knew that he was somehow aware of the fact that I had been doing it deliberately, and he knew that it would eventually help the both of us in the long run. Unfortunately, his actions said a completely different story.

After having driven him away, Shuie took to the bottle. He would, on numerous occasions, go to parties and end up crying, all the while whispering my name to himself. All this was related to me by mutual friends who would then, in turn, feel sorry for Shuie and again ask me exactly *why* I had decided to leave him.

“Things were getting kind of boring.” I would say to some of them. “We’d been together for quite a long time, you know? I just felt like I needed something more adventurous.”

“I can’t see myself having any future with him.” I would say to others. “We’re still quite young and I don’t want our relationship to become a hindrance to my career.”

After a while, my answers were fuelled more by agitation than honesty, and I would say something like, “I just wanted to sleep with more guys. You know what I mean, right? Monogamy’s far too overrated.” Perhaps just to see the shock on their faces.

Having looked back and considered my reasons for leaving him, I couldn’t help but feel that if anything, I owed Shuie an apology. After all, I hadn’t really had a concrete or cognizable reason for breaking up with him, but there just weren’t two ways about it.

Some things in life simply refused to follow the logic or reason of propriety. If it wasn't right, it just wasn't right, and when you followed what your heart said, you were bound to hurt others in the process.

If only Shuie had not been a nice guy. All this would've been so much easier to explain to myself and to others.

Amidst all this reminiscing, an unexpected call came from my Mother. First Prabhu, now my mom? I 'wondered' what she wanted to talk to me about.

"Richa," she began. "I want you to carefully think twice about what you're going to do."

"Ma, who told you?" I said, quietly brimming with rage. Where had my privacy gone? What was the point of living alone in an apartment if I couldn't even make a simple decision by myself without having a hundred people call to give advice?

"Prabhu called. He told me everything. He thinks it would be extremely 'moronic' of you to go, and if you do go, he told me to tell you that he never wants you to contact him again. Personally, I don't know. I just want you to think twice about what you're going to do."

"If I go, I should not contact Prabhu ever again? That's extremely childish, Ma. How could you condone something like that?"

"I'm not condoning anything. He told me to tell you something, and I did. I just want you to remember all those nights you would call me and cry about the stupid decision that you had made. It lasted for God knows how long, remember?"

"Hmm."

"You've come a long way since then. Don't go and throw it all away. I understand that youth and love are wonderful things, I mean, I too was in love once, so I know. I also know that nothing should take precedence over the security of your future. Mental, financial, physical, everything! Security is always the first criteria to guide your decisions, right?"

"Don't you think I've made quite a few bad decisions already though?"

"Well, it's never too late to change that. I just don't want you to cry so much again, baby. These things take a toll on a mother, no?"

"Sure, Ma. Thank you for being there. I'll make sure to do the right thing." And that was the end of our conversation.

As I cut the call, I stared at my phone screen for a long time. My wallpaper was a sketch of me, drawn and completed with uncouth and almost distressing lines.

Why was this my wallpaper? Why hadn't I changed it in such a long time if I didn't even like it? Perhaps because he had drawn it for me, and some part of me was still holding on to him. I should've killed that part of me by now. I should've deleted his number. I shouldn't have wasted the entire day thinking about him. But like I said — logic was not the heart's strong suit.

I went ahead and took off Kiran's stilettos to put on my muddy black heels. After all, three years ago, they'd been his gift to me on my twenty-first birthday. Despite their decrepit state, I felt that he would appreciate it if I wore them today. He was never one to care for appearances anyway.

It was still raining heavily outside. Clad in my summer dress and my black heels, I sent him a text message:

Hey, sure, sounds like fun. Give me your address. I'll be there in an hour. I might be a bit wet though, hope that's not a problem.

I had finally made my decision.

*

For the past two hours, I have witnessed an indecisive woman pace in and about me. I have never seen Richa so incredibly stressed before.

Now she's gone, but for all her confusion, I don't think she went anywhere special. After all, she took off her nice green shoes to wear those dirty black ones. Plus, she wore that flimsy dress in this weather!

Maybe she wants to catch a cold, maybe she's rebelling for the sake of rebelling.

For all the knowledge that I have gathered since my construction, and having already seen several lives pass me by, I sometimes wonder whether what I perceive as a daft and unseemly decision, could perhaps actually be the best one for that person to take. Only time will tell.

But speaking from experience, I'm quite certain that Richa too will one day disappear, but I'll always remember her pacing in and about me, talking on her phone, wearing that summer dress.

A room simply never forgets. Even though people just might, a room never forgets.

Sandal the Snowman

It was that time of the year again. Snow fell, covering the ground, and once more I took form in the Agnew household's front yard. I was Sandal the snowman who visited this family every single year for Christmas.

I'd been named Sandal seven years ago in honour of my namesake, a Rottweiler who'd jumped out of the Agnew mansion's third-floor window in a questionably delirious attempt to fly. I often wondered if his soul had continued to live within me... but unlike Sandal the dog, I was a lot more conscious of my limitations.

My physical body comprised of two broken buttons for eyes, twigs for arms, and a large snowball below my head to make moving around a little easier — though, until today, I'd never felt the need to let it take me anywhere.

It had all started over lunch. I'd eavesdropped on Ingrid Agnew, the middle daughter who would not stop talking about her visit to the *La Concha* beach in Spain during spring break. Fond stories about the sun and the sand had tickled my curiosity, and I imagined myself basking in the sunshine with my family, getting that same magical, swarthy tan Ingrid kept rambling on about.

For the first time in many, many years, I tried to consciously focus on rotating my bottom snowball. I wasn't sure if it was the weather, if my snow had acquired a bit of sludge, or mould, or if there was a clog in the gears, but I was simply unable to move. Was I suddenly too old to travel? Perhaps my grandkids, if I had any, would say so. But despite this, I did not give up. The greatest virtue for anyone, I imagined, was to visualize and vehemently believe in the image on the other side of their struggles. To believe in it with sincere intensity and to not give up until that blurry image became crystal clear, until it was more than a possibility, until it was really real. My enthusiasm was persistent — eventually, it enabled me to overcome my dormancy, and soon, I was off.

I travelled toward Heathrow Airport. Although my fellow snowmen found brilliant comedy in my itinerary, they were a lot more helpful with directions than humans, who would turn a deaf ear to any inquiries from Sandal the travelling snowman.

I marvelled at these humans and their unknowing prejudice. It was tremendously foolish to presume that snowmen were automatically daft creatures. Snowmen were not creatures at all, but in fact, a singular entity — all of us connected by the cold white sand.

"Excuse me, ma'am?" I asked a beautiful young snowgirl. "Could you point me towards Heathrow Airport?" She twisted her head, her sharp carrot nose pointing me towards my destination.

It took the assistance of three snowmen, two snowgirls, and one forgotten block of ice for me to finally reach the airport, six hours after I had first embarked upon my journey.

Now at the airport, I found myself facing a new quandary — in order to get to San Sebastian, I would have to buy a ticket. For a ticket, I would need one-eighty pounds. I did not have one-eighty pounds, which happened to thoroughly vex the ticket agent.

I regretted not having borrowed any cash for my vacation from Jonathan Agnew. He doubtless would not have refused if I had asked him nicely enough. Now, however, it was too late.

I decided to turn back and head home when suddenly a voice yelled out to me. "You there!

Snowman, what's your name?" It was a man clad in a *Ryanair* suit.

"Sandal" I replied.

"Where are you heading?"

"San Sebastian, but I don't have enough cash."

"One of our planes is set to depart in an hour, but the heating's all wonky. We decorated the entire plane with Christmas trees, fake snow, gifts, and socks to justify the temperature, but we need a snowman to complete the illusion. What do you say?"

"Depends. Where're you heading?"

"Tenerife."

"Tenerife? Does it have a beach?"

"Sandal, why, it's got one of the best!" exclaimed the suit.

During the five-hour flight, I could hear a few adults complain about the low temperature. I failed to see what they were on about, considering my journey up until then had been nothing but comfortable. Unfortunately, of course, this comfort was short-lived.

Once the passengers were permitted to unfasten their seatbelts, I became quite a popular attraction for quite a few children on the plane. They approached me as though they had known me all their lives. Some targeted my face with fake snowballs. Some rubbed my belly. A particularly naughty lad stole one of my eyes. It gave me something to complain about as well, but before I could allow myself to get all heated-up, the pilot announced that we had reached Tenerife island.

We landed. I went through customs. Once I left the airport, I jumped into an SUV cab. "To the best beach in Tenerife!" I told him enthusiastically.

"Los Cristianos it is!" replied the driver, mimicking my jovial mood. However, once a few minutes passed, I started to develop the worst headache of my life. My high spirits began to fade when I realized that my arms had fallen off my body. I was melting.

"Take me to your closest beach," I said.

"Amigo, you're melting on my leather!' I heard the driver say. "I can't take you anywhere like this." That's when my other eye gave up on me and fell off.

I heard him open the car door and then felt his warm hands on my snow as he pulled me out. It took me three excruciatingly long hours to melt away and die.

When I finally awoke, I found myself standing in a long queue of snowmen, snowwomen, and snowchildren.

As the queue shortened, I heard the tired Snowmaster ask, "Where to?" to which all the snowpeople would respond with places like Calgary, Alaska, or Stockholm.

Soon, it was my turn, and the Snowmaster posed me the same question, "Where to?"

"Los Cristianos it is!" I replied with unwavering enthusiasm.

After that, a snow-intern guided me to a particular door. It was labeled 'Number Three'. Years later, I would continue to wonder – why door number three? Why not four, five, or even seven? What was so special; what was so significant about that particular number? But at that moment...

"Through here." Said the snow-intern, and through the door, I went.

On the other side, my bottom snowball rolled against prickling and tickling sand. I continued to move forward until I could feel the waves hit my belly. The sun shone bright and felt wonderful against my glossy snow cheeks.

Los Cristianos, was I in a dream? I couldn't wait to tell the Agnew family about my experience next Christmas. And if I ever managed to meet Sandal the dog, I would finally ask him the question burning in my soul.

"Sandal, my friend. Tell me, what did you find when you took the chance to dream a little?"

Stuffed

It looked at me every day but I didn't mind.
Deep down in this beating heart of mine,
I knew that if anyone in this world cared for me, it would be him.

I could see my entire life reflect in front of me in those big brown beautiful eyes.
Maybe I was wrong.
What if I went out and searched for that place where I belonged?
What if, someone did find me and I, someone?
Wouldn't that feel oh so right?

He was stuffed with cotton,
I was stuffed with thoughts.
And they were slowly feeding on my mind.
Like I was his host,
And he, my parasite.

Or was it the other way around?
“I don't think so.” We reply.

I wear my favourite dress.
Sit in front of him.
Kiss his furry, little, irresistible cheek, and escape through the front door.
I’m going to find love,
Never to come home again,
I bid him farewell.

He was stuffed with cotton,
I, stuffed with thoughts.

When We Sleep Together

I could remember my head beginning to throb when Anandi, my baby sister, plucked the T.V. remote out of my hands for the umpteenth time. The pulsing migraine had only fuelled my agitation. All I'd wanted to do was snatch the remote back and return to watching the latest music videos of all the upcoming European bands on VH1. At the time, she had been six and I, eleven.

Our fights over the television came to an end soon after that. In retrospect, I missed those simple days when we were just so free of responsibility. (A year after this, I would get sent away to boarding school courtesy of a mildly violent altercation with my Mathematics professor during Trigonometry class.)

But back in that moment… when I snatched the remote from her hands, Anandi had wailed dramatically because she'd always been a capricious little time-bomb. A bitterness suffused my mouth. I'd often envied her ability to turn on the waterworks like a tap. What a waste of tears and energy. Nobody wanted to listen to this dull baritone nattering on about blue whales on the National Geographic.

Anandi's sorrowful sobs came to an abrupt halt when it became eclipsed by our Mother's livid scolding. I'd been thankful that both of us had been on the receiving end of the lecture and not just me alone, as the case had often been whenever we'd gotten into a scuffle.

Mother had pulled the plug on the television and immediately sent us to our room. She'd also revoked our 'one-hour-television-after-dinner' license for the week that followed. This had only deepened my animosity towards Anandi. As much as I'd tried, I couldn't imagine the responsibility for this pointless situation falling on anyone but Anandi and her idiotic love for animals on the National Geographic.

After this entire episode with Mother, Anandi and I had sat silently on our beds and unabashedly fumed at each other. The silence that'd filled the room had been a true testament to our mutual hostility.

I could remember focusing my thoughts on sleeping since it'd been getting pretty late, but then deciding otherwise. There had been something about that night. Something that had beckoned me; it had lured me with stories full of enchantment and intimacy. Stories that I could never rationalize, but they had, in the end, only remained stories. Their mystery had only ever manifested in the form of me resorting to comic books, or video games if I'd been feeling lazier.

An expression of uneasiness had crossed Anandi's face when I'd picked up my comic book. It had been a graphic novel by Vishwajyoti Ghosh, titled *Delhi Calm.* The book focused on life during the Emergency period in India, and the subject matter had been something unquestionably out of my depth.

Anandi's breathing had gotten louder and louder. Her scrupulous stare had penetrated both me and Ghosh's characters, clearly to engender a reaction; However, I hadn't been ready to give her the satisfaction just yet.

"I'm feeling sleepy," she'd said. I'd automatically switched the room lights off and the bedside lamp on. From the corner of my eye, I could see that her face had remained unchanged. She showed no signs of going to sleep anytime soon. The now single source of light in the room furthered the plaintiveness in Anandi's eyes — they'd been quite hard to withstand, but I had never been one to give up so easily. *When I picked a battle, I would fight it to the end. No other way around it.*

For the first time in that juvenile squabble of ours, I had felt like the one in control. At the same time, I could remember realizing how pathetic it was to exert this power over my own baby sister.

Her age and innocence shone in her eyes — a lamp-light in their own right — when she fearfully said, "Aren't you going to sleep? I don't want to go to the *Undulating World* all on my own."

A newfound interest had piqued within me at the unfamiliar term. When I'd asked Anandi what she had meant by 'The Undulating World', she had reacted with genuine consternation at my lack of awareness.

"It's where we go when we sleep," she informed me quite matter of factly. "A world that hides under our dreams."

Upon noticing my total cluelessness about the topic, she proceeded to elaborate.

Her friend Jamila had first described her fear of the *Undulating World* during the walk home from school. She'd told Anandi to never take her elder brother for granted, for it would be he who'd probably protect her from the demons in this foreboding land.

"Demons?" I repeated with equal parts curiosity and confusion.

"Well, no one has ever seen them, but the legend goes that they make their presence felt in an extremely obvious manner."

"And how's that?" I'd asked.

Upon hearing my question, Anandi sat up straight on the bed and took in a deep breath, as though prepping to delve into a story that would consume all of the night. I'd played the part of the eager child who'd maintain pin-drop silence while the storyteller did what she had to do.

"Once upon a time there were two people, a boy, and a girl. They both loved each other lots and lots, and to keep their love alive, they would sleep together, and consequently enter the Undulating World together as well.

"Over time, the boy naturally grew skeptical about the existence of demons. He began to think that the entire idea of the Undulating World was complete bogus. It became something of an inconvenience to him. Why? I don't know. Maybe he wanted to read a comic book like you, but it might be something else entirely. No one knows.

"One night, as an experiment, the boy played possum until the girl fell asleep. Afterwards, he decided to stay awake. He wanted to see what would happen. If there truly were demons in the Undulating World, surely he would see a sign, and if that were to happen, he would immediately go to sleep and save his love.

"And so began the longest night of the boy's life. He waited for hours, but there were neither any hints of danger nor any indication from the girl that something bad was happening to her. 'Finally,' he thought to himself. 'I've debunked this stupid lie that we continue to tell ourselves! There are no demons! There is no Undulating World!' He felt restless pride surge through him as he waited for the girl to wake up. He couldn't wait to tell his love how naïve they had been. All this time they had slept together in fear of something that did not exist. But the girl did not wake up.

"The boy tried everything! He pushed her, he threw water on her face, he even dropped some in her ears. He yelled her name as loud as he could. Countlessly, he tried to fall asleep, hoping that he'd find his lost love and bring her back home. But when he would wake, she would still be asleep.

"The boy cried and cried in endless lament. He held onto a single string of hope and refused to give up until there was simply nothing left to do. He felt like a fool to have left his love all alone in the Undulating World. Surely the demons had gotten to her by now. If only he had been by her side. He could have protected his love, and the girl would have never been lost."

And thus concluded the story of the two lovers. Anandi's soprano voice had reached an abrupt and uninviting end. Her shrill voice usually stung me, but at that time, it had been the silence that was deafening.

I placed my graphic novel on the shelf next to my bed. '*The Emergency can wait,*' I thought to myself. '*Right now, I need to protect my baby sister*'.

I switched off the bedside lamp.

"Don't worry Anandi," I said, curling under the covers. "As long as I'm here, you'll never have to go to the Undulating World alone. As your big brother, I will protect you, no matter what."

I could sense Anandi smile, even though it was impossible for me to see anything in the darkness.

"Thank you," she whispered. Those were the last words I had heard before we both fell asleep.

*

I woke up next to Drishti on a cold Saturday morning. Both of us were tucked comfortably under our maroon blanket. Seventeen years had passed since the night I'd first heard about the world hiding under our dreams. A land that wasn't just our own, but communal in a very familiar yet unsettling manner. At twenty-eight years, one couldn't dwell too much on such fantasies. The modern world was fast-paced. To survive it meant to sustain an image that kept in tune with the times. A world like this did not allow us the time to linger in fairytales.

For my initial years at boarding school, Anandi had often written me emails. In one such email, she'd related to me that Jamila had been going through a pretty rough time. Her parents had decided to get a divorce. Jamila had blamed the separation on the fact that her parents almost never slept together.

Realistically speaking, it made complete sense. However, if one looked at it through the eyes of the story, it seemed borderline nonsensical.

But our ironic hearts loved to work in nonsensical ways. They would always choose the most ridiculous path for us to follow, and the path would often lead us straight into the raging fire... but the journey would be beautiful, the path strewn with sweet-smelling flowers and incense, the mud soft under our feet; the experience would never be one worth missing. For humans, for the unaware and emotionally- incapable species that we were, a jovial stroll into the fire always sounded like a great idea.

Drishti's face was so close to mine. She was beautiful. As the images of the Undulating World pervaded through my brain, I couldn't help but wonder when Drishti had come to bed last night.

It was easy for me to convince myself, that she'd deliberately left me alone to face the demons dwelling surreptitiously under my dreams. Last night I had survived, but how much longer would I be able to sustain this? Where had she been? Was she secretly helping someone else in the Undulating World?

Thankfully, logic suddenly retook precedence and I realized how insane my thoughts would seem to any self-respecting adult. I told myself that there was nothing to worry about. 'She could have been working late. Her phone battery could have died. Perhaps she went out for a couple of drinks with her friends.' There were innumerable ways to justify her absence, and all of them were definitely more plausible than my fairytale. I let go of the thought before it could take complete control and instead decided to make breakfast. Saturday special, Drishti's favourite, french toast with hot sausages and vanilla coffee.

*

"Oh, god, just stop already!" Drishti yelled. "Do you even hear yourself? Undulating World and whatnot? Why can't you just say it straight?" Her eyes narrowed dangerously. "*Drishti, are you sleeping with someone else!* Isn't that what you are asking?"

All I could do was stare at our neglected breakfast. How could I have allowed things to get this bad? At the back of my mind, I kicked myself for bringing up her absence last night. Technically, she hadn't been absent. She had playfully pointed this out to me initially, before the storm. This was certainly true because she did eventually end up in bed next to me.

Only, it had been after I'd already fallen asleep. A small technicality, but possibly a grave one.

"I'm sorry. I suppose I just got a bit insecure, that's all." Is what I should have said. I should have smiled a bit, given her a warm hug and then taken her to the table where a lavish breakfast awaited. The morning meal had been prepared with the best of ingredients and a lot of love.

"Look," is what I really said. "It's not about whether you slept with someone else or not. I…"

I wasn't able to find the right words to convince her of my concern, of my fear of being left alone in a world that only existed when we sleep.

"I just wanted you to be there when I had fallen asleep," I said.

"So that we could be together in the Undulating World," repeated Drishti in a strange undertone.

"Exactly!" I exclaimed enthusiastically. But upon spotting her expression of raging disbelief, I immediately realized my mistake.

This wasn't how I'd wanted my Saturday to unfold. Drishti already had one foot out the door. A few minutes ago, we'd been happy. There we had been, on my bed, lying side by side, faces a few inches from each other, that's what happiness looked and felt like... and now, thanks to some stupid tale my baby sister had told me years ago, everything had taken a turn for the worse.

"Won't you at least finish breakfast?" I asked plaintively.

Drishti flipped around, fuming at me. "You know, it's one thing to make excuses about your insecurities. But to bring your little sister into it! You should be ashamed!" And then, poof. Like an unwelcome magic trick. She was gone.

Two plates of French toast and hot sausage, and two cups of vanilla coffee were getting cold on my dining table. My appetite had abandoned me just like Drishti had. I had difficulty remembering why I'd decided to cook breakfast in the first place. No. Wait a second. It wasn't just the food. Everything seemed to be getting cold.

I thought I was losing my mind when I felt a firm presence grab me and try to crush me. I was enveloped in what felt like tepid and sticky clay. It felt like some strange ritual before my inevitable damnation.

As all my thoughts began to go haywire, I grew absolutely certain about one thing. If I slept alone tonight, nothing would let me escape the demons again. They were waiting for me. I could feel it in my gut.

I paced in my two-bedroom apartment. It was beautiful, with a wonderful little balcony, a kitchenette with a small dining area and a luxurious living room.

When I'd first bought it, everyone in my family had complained about its size. They claimed it was far too small a space to invest in. Now, as I paced through my apartment, I couldn't help but cower in the midst of this overwhelming space that I was the sole and lonely proprietor of.

For a short while, I panicked at the thought of falling prey to the demons... but it didn't persist for too long. Soon, I realized that the demons had already gotten to me. They'd already managed to separate me from the person I loved. I had been affected the same sorrowful fate that had resulted in the destruction of the lovers from Anandi's story.

I couldn't waste another second. I immediately picked up my cell phone and dialled Anandi's number. She was in her final year of college, and albeit she might've been busy, she was my last resort. She was the only one I could talk to about the Undulating World.

Anandi picked up my call after four rings. By the caustic tone of her voice, I conjectured that she'd probably had a few too many to drink last night. Doubtless, she would fall back to sleep as soon as this conversation was over. I couldn't ascertain whether or not she was happy to hear from me. Maybe she was only being polite because I was her brother. Nevertheless, I told her everything that had happened that morning. The grimy details of the fight along with every elusive and threatening thought that was tormenting me. I explained to her how Drishti hadn't been there when I'd gone to bed, so surely this must be it! The demons must have taken me! I did not give Anandi a chance to speak, but then again, she didn't make any attempts to interject either.

"Please, I don't know if it's too late! You've got to tell me if there's any way I can get myself out of this mess!"

There were a few seconds of silence. It was painful and felt like an eternity. I heard Anandi take a deep breath and mentally prepared myself for her response.

"Dada," she said slowly. "I don't know if you're just messing with me, or if you've actually lost your mind. I pray it's the former."

I couldn't believe what I was hearing. Had Anandi too acclimatized herself to the emotionless pace of the world? Had she too, allowed no room for belief in the story she'd herself once whispered to her elder brother? I felt like a relic, stuck in a time and space long gone by as the rest of the world overtook me, giving me no opportunity to catch up.

"But if what you're saying is actually true, and that is how you feel, then all I can say is that you never really understood the story. Now let me sleep. And next time, call me at a decent hour! It's ten in the morning on a Saturday!" And with that, our conversation came to an end.

The notion of youth was something very difficult for me to define. After a point in someone's life, there were certain changes a person was capable of making, and certain changes that a person wasn't. This was because *change* threatened to shake the entire foundation of their being. It meant the risk of losing their identity. As for me, I was unsure whether I would ever change my perspective on the story… but as Anandi had brought to my attention, *I did not know what the story actually meant.*

Outside, the sound of traffic was deafening. Where do people go on a Saturday morning? The noise peeved me beyond measure, and soon it developed a voice of its own. The voice kept reminding me that I was stuck, while the rest of the world continued to move on.

I walked up to the open window and shut it. My attempt to muffle the cacophony was futile, and the noise inside my head was only aggravated by it. Running out of insights and ideas, I figured that the best thing to do was to finish the meal I had so painstakingly prepared for me and my better half.

After the first sip of my coffee, the main door opened and in walked Drishti. I stood up from my chair just like a soldier would in deference to his commander. Without saying a word, or even caring to make eye contact, she came and sat down in front of me. She quietly tore little pieces of her French toast and ate it in a manner so as to avoid saying anything that might give away her feelings towards the breakfast I'd made.

She lifted her coffee cup.

"Wait!" I exclaimed before she could take a sip. I quickly added a teaspoon of sugar and stirred it. Once again, she drank it without reacting.

I too started to tear my French toast into bite-sized pieces. A truly unusual method. Never before had I eaten French toast in such a fashion, but I was too distracted by Drishti to think too much about it.

As I awaited a response from her, I realized that the sound of the traffic wasn't bothering me anymore. Neither was the cold air pinching at my skin. Compared to five minutes ago, I was definitely feeling far more at ease.

"I'm sorry I acted out in the morning," she finally said. "I should've called you yesterday and told you that I was going to be late. I didn't even go anywhere right now. I was just sulking downstairs. Next time, could you please just directly ask me whatever you want to ask. Don't spiral around in circles." She paused and took another sip of coffee. "And please don't make up stupid stories like the one you did today. Okay?"

"I'm sorry," I replied. "I suppose I just got a bit insecure, that's all."

The rest of the morning was spent eating in comfortable silence. A warmth suffused me as I sat opposite the woman I loved and enjoyed my breakfast.

Fantasy can never be reality, and reality can never be fantasy, yet each is a reflection of itself.

For the first time in seventeen years, I realized that I had finally seen what the Undulating World looked like.

Jarvi the Pianist - Hill of Lost Hope

"I'm thinking about a comeback," I told the giraffe conversationally. Certainly, he wasn't an *actual* giraffe — if one turned a blind eye to the giraffe head, from the waist down, he appeared to be a rather handsome young man.

"A comeback, eh?" The giraffe mused. "How long has it been? Fifteen years? I doubt Jarvi the pianist has remained all that fresh in people's memories." He tilted his head to crack the muscles in his long neck.

His concern, while valid, was harsh, and I curled around my gin and tonic. "Why a giraffe?" I asked, not particularly curious, but eager to change the topic. I had never done well with negative criticism.

The giraffe countered, "Why a comeback?"

I thought about it. “I’m not sure.” I took a sip. “I’m afraid that if I don’t do it, I might actually lose my mind.”

“Lose your mind?” The giraffe made a face. “Seems a bit extreme. What, you scared of going senile in your old age or something?”

My lips twisted. “No. Well, not exactly.” I tried to describe it. “It’s the music. I need to make music. I’ve been away from it for too long. Without this album, I’d just be an old man, sitting in front of a television, seeing nothing, hearing nothing… being nothing. It’s the last thing I want for myself.”

“Well, then,” he said, not very interested in the sob story. “How’s it looking?”

“Well,” I responded, trying to sound jovial. “I have the first verse for the first song, so I guess that’s progress?”

He hummed, and we fell silent for a moment.

Then the giraffe downed the remainder of his lager. “‘Why?’ is not the right question you should ask.”

“Pardon?” I said, confused.

“You’d inquired earlier,” he reminded me. “‘Why a giraffe?’ It’s not a matter of ‘why’. I was always a giraffe. Unfortunately, they put me in the body of a human.” A bitter laugh erupted from his lips. “The other kids would bully me for being different. I had a human’s face, but it didn’t help when I *knew* my soul was that of a giraffe's. Kids had a particular eye for things that made people different."

"Doesn't sound like a very happy childhood," I said, unsure of how to respond.

"It wasn't," he agreed. "But things changed after I put on the mask. The bullying stopped. The name-calling didn't end, but it became easier to ignore it. For the first time in my life, I could feel the differences within me disappearing. I was who I was, who I am today."

"So you're wearing a mask, then?" I asked curiously.

"Well," he said dryly. "After the surgery, I'd say it's a pretty damn permanent one."

He polished off his drink, placed some money on the table and took his leave, bidding a warm goodbye to both myself and Ria, the genial bartender who approached to take the payment.

Giving Ria a friendly smile, I ordered another gin and tonic, looking back down at the notebook that had spawned my whole conversation with the giraffe. A couple of lines were scrawled across the page. Some of them — the ones with potential — were marked with little asterisks.

Well, I'm nothing but a traveller,
In a world that's passed me by,
Like a dancing singing zombie,

Who'll play some chords in his free time.

I sighed.

"Have you ever been to the Hill of Lost Hope?" A voice suddenly asked. I looked up to see Ria knowingly nodding at the depressingly empty notebook as she placed my drink on the coaster.

My eyebrows furrowed. "Is that a real place or…?"

"Don't know," she shrugged. "That's what the locals call it. I've never been there myself, but I think it might be a fun place to visit. If you're looking for some inspiration, that is."

Curiosity rose within me. "Really? Why's that?"

"Well," she paused. "It's got some really great stories." Her eyes twinkled with mischief and her voice took on a mystical edge. "The place apparently has some serious vibes, you know what I mean? Locals talk about how the line between life and death gets super blurry over there, and how dead souls can breathe life on the hill after midnight. One of the aunties told me that if you went there after 12 o'clock, you might even chance upon a couple of them." She shrugged again. "Or at least, that's how the story goes."

My mouth tugged into a grin. "I never took you for someone who'd take stock in an old wives' tale."

"Oh," she snorted. "I think the whole thing's complete bull. But for you artist-types, it might be a good place to check out, right? If a hill full of spirits isn't inspirational enough for you, I just don't know what is."

"True," I agreed. I checked my thirty-year-old Seiko. "You said after midnight, right?" It was half-past one in the morning, and I figured it was worth a shot.

"Good luck on your comeback!" she said, cheerfully accepting the money I handed her. "I imagine you'll need it." She'd clearly been eavesdropping on the conversation from earlier, but I surprisingly didn't mind.

(Eight months ago, I too would've laughed at the prospect of a comeback. But then something happened. Fate intervened — the decision had already been made for me. I had to do it. And it wasn't just born from the fear of becoming redundant. It wasn't about reminding people I still existed, or about competing with whatever people were listening to these days, or even making this for the handful of fans I still had left… if there were any, to begin with. I was doing this for me.)

I gave her one final smile before departing for *The Hill of Lost Hope.*

I'll be walking to the edge of my life,
For entertainment purposes,
I could use my imagination,

But how? When I've broken all my compasses.

I found it quite intriguing that Ria had referred to them as *spirits*, instead of *ghosts*. I preferred the former over the latter. It might have had something to do with the protracted influence of mainstream horror.

'Ghosts' had a bit of an ominous ring to it. To me, 'ghosts' had become synonymous to evil, fear, unfulfilled desires. 'Spirits', on the other hand, felt more meditative, calming, and complete.

I did not believe in ghosts, I realized, but a convincing argument could be made for spirits as well. Which begged the question: Was this about inspiration, or was I looking for a sign — or rather, *someone*, in this ludicrous quest of mine?

"If she's there," I muttered to myself. "If I see her… this quest. This album. It all ends."

I considered the whole notion of spirits. Of why they lingered. According to most arguments, spirits had chosen to do so to be close to their loved ones. According to others, spirits had no choice at all. Rather, they were bound by something that refused to release them. I wondered if spirithood came with consequences, no matter if they had chosen it or had been chosen by it.

My trousers got soaked as I walked through a shallow stream, which then led to a sudden uphill climb.

The journey was quiet in the emptiness of the night, and her name continued to ring in my head. In the sound of her voice. *Sara.*

More than anything, I wanted the chance to be with her again. Preferably forever.

On the Hill of Lost Hope,
I hope to find everything that I've lost,
You see I'm dead as dead could be,
But I'm sure someone's far more dead than me.

As my feet sank into the mud, I couldn't help but fondly look back at the time I had proposed to her. Her parents had not fancied the idea of her marrying a musician. They'd wanted someone more stable, more secure, someone, with a guaranteed monthly paycheque; not that she needed the support of someone else's paycheque — at the time, Sara had been months away from becoming a full-fledged dentist. Or as she liked to call it, an 'odontologist'.

Sara and I had met at a bar in arguably the worst way possible. I had been celebrating the release of my second studio album, *A Siesta before the Feast*. My business relationship with the studio drummer had soured, and, perhaps in retaliation, he'd slipped the hard H into my drink.

Soon after, I'd lost complete consciousness. Upon waking, I had found myself in the empty parking lot behind the pub with a lubricated tube stuffed down my throat. When I opened my eyes, the first thing I saw was her. Sara. The crowd surrounding us had been nothing more than background noise.

The way her face had hovered over mine… it had felt as though she'd been my guardian angel. She'd breathed a sigh of relief before systematically extracting the tube from my throat. Needless to say, it hadn't been a pleasant experience.

I'd thanked Sara for what she had done for me, and had been determined to repay the favour. As it had turned out, she'd been a big fan of my first studio album, *Hear Wolves Play Jazz.* In return for my life, I gave her an autograph, and we exchanged numbers.

I could remember her voice as clear as day. "Well then," she'd said sheepishly. The crowd had slowly begun to disperse once they'd realized that the excitement had ended. "Should I be expecting to hear from Jarvi the pianist?"

"I doubt I'll call you," I'd said to her cheekily, and a startled laugh had burst from her lips.

"Oh, really? And why's that?"

"Twenty-nine years have made me very sure of who I am," I'd grinned. "Trust me when I say this: no matter how hard I try not to; I'm definitely going to lose your number."

"Twenty-nine, huh?" She'd tucked a lock of hair behind her ears. "I guess that gives me three more years to achieve that same level of self-awareness."

I'd gone for it. "Why don't you come back to my place and maybe I could help you with that?"

Her eyebrows had risen at the offer. "Okay," she'd agreed. "But first it might be nice if you got cleaned up."

And that's when I'd looked down and realized that I had been utterly drenched in my own puke. Sara had broken into a cute little laugh. She should have walked away. If a meter for the romance between us had existed, it should have shown negatives. But for some unfathomable reason, there she had been, an hour later, with me, in my apartment.

That night, we hadn't slept. I'd thrown open the doors to my record library and she'd helped herself to the choices. The first album she picked: *Different Class* by *Pulp.*

"Not a lot of people know about *Pulp* in India." I'd remarked.

"How do you know about a lot of people?" had been her retort.

"Fair enough. I guess I just meant that a lot of my friends don't know about *Pulp*."

"Maybe you have the wrong friends."

"Wow, now who's being judgemental?"

"Hey, I'm just trying to keep up with you."

We stayed awake, chatting, taking turns playing one record after another. *Kate Bush. Brian Eno. The Pixies.*

"Won't it be a problem heading to the hospital if you're sleep-deprived?" I'd asked at around six in the morning.

"Not on Sundays. Day off."

"What about the people who fall sick on Sundays?"

"I doubt they're going to miss an intern. Especially an odontology intern."

"That's the tooth genre, right?"

"It's a science," she'd said amusedly. "Not a video game. Or a piece of music. But yes, it's the tooth genre."

"No offence intended," I'd said.

"No offence taken," she'd replied.

Come morning, we'd had breakfast together. She made me eggs, sunny-side up, and a cup of hot coffee. The best I'd ever had. When she'd walked out the door, I hadn't known if I'd ever see her again. Over the years, I'd happily seen a lot of girls leave through that door, but Sara, I'd somehow known, was different.

I'd wanted to be with her. I'd wanted to have more conversations with her about hospitals and music. I'd have been happy talking to her about moisturizer for all I cared; it was just her voice that I had wanted in my ears. I had just wanted her to be there.

But being a twenty-nine-year-old, slightly depressed musician, I'd done nothing about it.

Like the girl I'd lost to cancer,
When deceased she ceased to be,
Or have I got it upside down?
For there you are,
While I am,
Nowhere to be found.

I reached the top of the hill. The view of the city was mesmerizing. Amazed by the bright and beautiful lights below me, I felt twenty-two and eager to grasp the world within my fingertips, all over again.

I looked around, trying to milk the view for inspiration. I also looked around, unable to help myself, in search for even the slightest hint of a spirit.

I had no plan. If, perchance, I actually managed to stumble across one, what would I even say? *Excuse me, do you happen to be dead? Can you commune with other dead people? Would you happen to know where I can find my late wife, Sara?*

I doubted the feasibility of that scenario — I mean, if they couldn't even find their way to the afterlife, how'd they know where to find my wife?

I lit a cigarette. Took a swig out of my flask. It was gin and tonic.

Two weeks after we'd first met, Sara and I had made love for the first time. For the first week, I'd tried really hard to put her out of my mind. I'd failed. Miserably. The following Monday, I'd decided to give her a call. Exactly as predicted, I'd managed to lose her phone number. However, in an unprecedented twist, those seven digits had left a strong enough imprint on my memory.

She'd been busy through the week. On Saturday, we'd gone to the theatre to catch a cheesy Bollywood film and laugh to our heart's content. After that, we'd had dinner at a new Chinese restaurant where we talked more about cinema.

She'd come back with me to my apartment, and just like last time, we'd listened to some music, after which we'd proceeded to the bedroom where we had made our own music under the sheets.

On Sunday morning, as we'd lain half-asleep in bed, I'd asked her if she'd like to get married. She didn't think twice about it and had said yes.

I took another swig from my flask. I was nearing the end of my third cigarette and was yet to encounter any spirits.

I was just starting to get a tad bit bored when suddenly, out of nowhere, I heard a man yell from somewhere far away. I looked around and saw no one in sight. The distant yells continued. I walked to the edge of the hill and there he was, on the other side of the stream, vigorously gesturing at me to come down.

This man made no attempt to climb up the hill. His whole tone and body language screamed that he was scared — not for himself, but for me, though it was difficult to ascertain why. I exhausted my cigarette and looked around again before deciding that the trip, although purposeless, had been fun enough, and started making my way back down.

And then something happened, and it happened really fast.

I heard an otherworldly growl coming from behind me. I turned around and just barely caught a glimpse of *something* before it barrelled right into me. Next thing I knew, I was catapulting off the ground and violently hurtling down the hill, which now seemed a lot steeper than it had been when I'd climbed it.

It was a spirit. A woman. She had a translucent white glow and even though she was physically small, the sheer strength I had felt suggested that she was far more than she seemed. She stared at me as I continued my painful descent. "That better not be you, Sara." I thought to myself.

Just before I fell into the stream, her figure disappeared without a single goodbye, and suddenly it felt as though she had never even been there.

Don't laugh at my situation, honey,
I promised it's just a phase,
Or am I going oh so completely insane?
As I dream of forgotten days.

I hit the surface of the stream with a loud splash. It felt like I was drowning in the middle of the ocean, which was odd considering how shallow the stream had seemed when I'd previously walked through it. Crimson suffused the crystal clear water as it sparkled under the moonlight. What was happening? Was this real? Was I imagining things?

No, it was definitely real. I felt an excruciating pain in my chest; it felt like I'd cracked a few ribs. My left leg felt completely mangled, though I couldn't make out too much of it in the blur of the water. And if this didn't seem bad enough, I was losing more and more blood with each second I spent under. Where exactly was this blood spewing from? I had no idea, but it didn't seem very likely that I had a lot of time left.

I fell deeper and deeper into the abyss. There was no end to it, and even if there was, I doubted that I'd still be alive to meet it.

Sara. Her voice once again rang through my ears. There was a piercing feeling in my heart, almost as if a long needle had been pushed through it. I knew what this pain was. It was the hurt of leaving something unfulfilled.

"Doesn't look like I'll be making that comeback after all," I said to myself, letting the words disappear into the water. But then to my surprise, I heard a voice whisper back to me.

"Shh… are you actually going to give up that easily?"

Her voice. There it was, yet again. Except this time, it had an absurd amount of reverb.

"Easily? Can you not see the state I'm in?" I replied to the voice.

"I see it," she said. "You going to let me help you out?"

"Oh," I said, now feeling completely delirious. "First you put me here. Then you want to help me? You're a real tough nut to crack, Sara, you know that?"

"Hey," she said, with what sounded like a smile. "I'm just trying to keep up with you."

"That gem again," I couldn't help but grin.

And then without any warning, something akin to a cricket bat swung across my face and pretty much broke it. Obviously, I blacked out.

When I finally awoke, half of my body was submerged in the stream. The man from earlier stood by my head, doing nothing, being nothing, simply blankly staring down at me. My leg wasn't mangled anymore, but I still had broken ribs to deal with. Blood poured out of an ugly laceration on my abdomen, but it was nothing unsurvivable.

"I came down," I said to the man. "You happy?"

He said something in Kannada and left. It probably hadn't been anything pleasant. I got back up, pain stinging in my chest and abdomen, and began to make my way back home. As my feet sank into the mud, and the water dripped from my hair into my eyes, the words swam into my head — the finishing touches to a song I would later decide to call 'The Hill of Lost Hope'.

Your hand is on my cheek,
Your eyes look into mine,
I worry you're here to say goodbye,
But you softly whisper in your tender voice,
'My dear Jarvi, I'm afraid, that it's yet not your time to die.'

www.ingramcontent.com/pod-product-compliance
Lightning Source LLC
Chambersburg PA
CBHW050023170726
48282CB00025B/516
* 9 7 8 9 3 5 3 6 1 4 8 9 8 *